The Raven

A Haunting Meditation on Loss, Madness & the Echo of "Nevermore"

A Modern Translation

Adapted for the Contemporary Reader

Edgar Allan Poe

Translated by Tim Zengerink

Table of Contents

Preface
Message to the Reader

Rebuilding the Greatest Library in Human History

Thousands of years ago, the Library of Alexandria was the heart of global knowledge — a sanctuary where the wisdom of every known civilization was gathered and shared freely.

And then, it was lost.

Now, we're rebuilding it — and you are invited to join us.

At the Library of Alexandria, we've set out to make every book available to every person on Earth — not just in print, but in every language, every format, and for every reader.

Here's how we do it:

- **Deluxe Print Editions at True Printing Cost** - Order any book as a high-quality paperback, elegant hardcover, or stunning boxset — and only pay what it costs to print. No markups. No middlemen.
- **Unlimited Access to the Greatest Works** - Enjoy thousands of timeless classics — from Plato to Shakespeare to Tolstoy — in beautiful, modern eBook and audiobook editions. Read and listen without limits — for every reader, everywhere.
- **Modern Translations for Every Language & Dialect** - We're reimagining the classics in clear, accessible language — and translating them into every dialect imaginable. Everyone deserves to understand humanity's greatest ideas.

When you visit **LibraryofAlexandria.com**, you're not just accessing books — you're joining a global movement to restore, preserve, and share the wisdom of civilization.

Join us today at LibraryofAlexandria.com

Together, we'll ensure the light of human wisdom never fades again.

With gratitude,

The Modern Library of Alexandria Team

Visit:
www.libraryofalexandria.com
Or scan the code below:

Introduction

The Birth of a Literary Masterpiece

Edgar Allan Poe's *The Raven* (1845) stands as one of the most iconic and widely recognized poems in American literary history, a haunting narrative that captures the depths of grief, the creeping onset of madness, and the human yearning for answers in the face of loss. Its publication marked a turning point in Poe's career, catapulting him to fame and establishing him as a master of the macabre and the psychological. Written with meticulous attention to form, sound, and atmosphere, *The Raven* is not merely a poem about a man visited by a mysterious bird; it is a profound meditation on sorrow, memory, and the limits of human reason when confronted with the inescapable reality of death.

Poe himself considered *The Raven* a deliberate exercise in poetic technique and emotional effect. In his essay *The Philosophy of Composition*, published shortly after the poem's debut, he outlined the principles that guided its creation, claiming that every element—from the choice of refrain ("Nevermore") to the structure of its stanzas—was carefully calculated to produce a singular, unified emotional impact. While some critics have debated the extent to which this essay reflects Poe's actual process, it nevertheless offers valuable insights into the poet's belief that art should evoke an immediate and powerful response from its audience. For Poe, the ideal poem was one that blended musicality, melancholy, and beauty in a seamless whole, and The Raven is perhaps his finest realization of this ideal.

The narrative of *The Raven* is deceptively simple: a grieving narrator, mourning the loss of his beloved Lenore, is visited by a raven that perches above his chamber door and speaks a single, enigmatic word—"Nevermore." Over the course of the poem, the narrator's attempts to interpret this word lead him deeper into despair, as he projects his own fears and doubts onto the bird's repeated refrain. The raven, whether a supernatural messenger or merely a creature of instinct, becomes a mirror for the narrator's inner turmoil, reflecting back to him the hopelessness of his longing and the permanence of death. The poem's power lies in this interplay between external imagery and internal emotion, between the tangible presence of the raven and the intangible weight of grief.

Poe's use of language in *The Raven* is masterful, combining the musical qualities of rhyme, meter, and alliteration with a rich vocabulary of Gothic imagery. The poem is written in trochaic octameter, a meter that lends it a rhythmic, almost hypnotic quality, while the internal rhymes and refrains create a sense of echo and inevitability. Words such as "midnight dreary," "silken sad uncertain rustling," and "quaint and curious volume of forgotten lore" not only paint vivid pictures but also contribute to the poem's atmosphere of melancholy and mystery. This careful crafting of sound and sense is one of the reasons why The Raven remains so memorable and widely quoted.

The immediate success of the poem was extraordinary. Upon its publication in the *New York Evening Mirror*, *The Raven* captivated readers and critics alike, quickly spreading through newspapers and magazines across the country. Poe, who had long struggled for financial stability, finally found himself a literary celebrity. However, this fame was tinged with irony, as the success of *The Raven* did not translate into significant financial reward. Still, the poem secured his place in the American literary canon, influencing countless poets, writers, and artists in the decades that followed.

Themes of Loss, Madness, and the Supernatural

At the heart of *The Raven* lies the theme of grief—specifically, the grief of a man who has lost the love of his life. Lenore, though barely described, becomes the focal point of the narrator's despair, a symbol of unattainable beauty and eternal absence. The poem captures the obsessive nature of mourning, the way in which memory and longing can consume the mind and blur the boundary between reality and imagination. As the narrator fixates on the raven's cryptic "Nevermore," he moves from curiosity to anger to a kind of desperate resignation, embodying the stages of grief in a compressed, dramatic arc.

The descent into madness is another central theme. While the raven may initially appear as a literal bird, its role in the poem is far more symbolic. It becomes a projection of the narrator's inner state, a dark embodiment of his fears and doubts. Each repetition of "Nevermore" deepens the narrator's sense of hopelessness, until he is no longer certain whether the bird speaks with supernatural knowledge or whether he is merely hearing the echo of his own despair. This ambiguity—between the external and the internal, the real and the imagined—is a hallmark of Poe's work, reflecting his fascination with the fragility of the human mind.

The supernatural element of *The Raven* adds to its eerie power. While the bird itself may be a natural creature, its midnight arrival, its placement above the "chamber door," and its solemn, prophetic utterance all suggest a connection to otherworldly forces. The poem invites readers to wonder whether the raven is a messenger from the afterlife, a symbol of fate, or simply a dark figment of the narrator's imagination. Poe's genius lies in maintaining this uncertainty, allowing the poem to operate on multiple levels—psychological, spiritual, and symbolic—simultaneously.

The word "Nevermore" itself is a key to understanding the poem's meaning. On the surface, it is merely the bird's refrain, a word it has learned by rote. But in the context of the narrator's questions—about Lenore, about the possibility of reunion in the afterlife—it takes on a devastating finality. Each repetition becomes a blow to the narrator's hope, a reminder that some losses are irreparable, that some questions have no comforting answers. This interplay between language and meaning, between the literal and the symbolic, is at the heart of the poem's enduring resonance.

Poe's Style and the Poem's Lasting Legacy

Poe's stylistic mastery in *The Raven* is evident not only in its musicality but also in its structure and symbolism. The poem's 18 stanzas build gradually in intensity, each one deepening the emotional and psychological tension. The use of internal rhyme—"And the silken, sad, uncertain rustling of each purple curtain"—creates a sense of continuity and flow, while the careful repetition of sounds and phrases reinforces the poem's central themes. Poe's ability to combine form and content so seamlessly is one of the reasons why *The Raven* remains a cornerstone of poetic craftsmanship.

The imagery of the poem is both vivid and deeply symbolic. The midnight setting, the dying embers of the fire, the rustling curtains, and the shadow of the raven all contribute to a mood of unease and foreboding. The raven itself, traditionally a symbol of death and ill omen, becomes a powerful emblem of the narrator's inner darkness. Its perch on the "bust of Pallas" (the Greek goddess of wisdom) suggests a tension between reason and madness, knowledge and despair. By placing the bird above a symbol of rational thought, Poe implies that grief and emotion can overwhelm even the most disciplined mind.

The influence of *The Raven* on literature and popular culture has been profound. It has inspired countless imitations, adaptations, and references in art, music, and film. From the works of writers like Charles Baudelaire and Vladimir Nabokov to the films of directors like Tim Burton, the shadow of Poe's raven looms large. Its refrain of "Nevermore" has entered the cultural lexicon, a shorthand for irrevocable loss and unanswerable questions. The poem's blend of Gothic atmosphere, psychological depth, and musical language has made it a touchstone for both literary scholars and casual readers.

For modern audiences, *The Raven* remains as compelling as it was in Poe's time. Its exploration of grief, memory, and the limits of reason speaks to universal human experiences, while its technical brilliance continues to inspire poets and writers. The poem invites us not only to feel the narrator's anguish but also to reflect on the nature of language, meaning, and the ways in which our own minds can both comfort and torment us. As you read The Raven, consider the layers of meaning that Poe has woven into its lines—the interplay of sound and sense, the blending of the real and the imagined, the tension between hope and despair. It is a work that rewards both emotional engagement and careful analysis, offering new insights with every reading.

The Poem

The Raven

On a gloomy midnight, as I sat thinking,
feeling weak and tired,
Over many a strange and fascinating
book of forgotten knowledge,
While I was nodding off, almost falling asleep,
suddenly there came a tapping sound,
As if someone was softly tapping,
tapping at my bedroom door.
"It's just some visitor," I muttered,
"tapping at my bedroom door—"

"Only this, and nothing more."

Ah, I clearly remember it was
during that harsh December,
And each dying ember cast
its ghostly shadow on the floor.
Eagerly I longed for tomorrow
—I had tried in vain to find
From my books, relief from grief
—grief for the lost Lenore—
For the rare and radiant maiden
whom the angels name Lenore—

Nameless here for evermore.

And the soft, melancholy,
hesitant rustling of each purple curtain
Thrilled me—filled me with incredible fears
I had never experienced before;
So that now, to calm the pounding of my heart,
I stood there repeating
"'It's just some visitor asking to come in
at my bedroom door"
Some late visitor requesting entry
at my bedroom door;—

"This is what it is, and nothing more."

Soon my spirit became bolder;
no longer filled with doubt,
"Sir," I said, "or Madam,
I truly beg for your forgiveness;
But the truth is I was sleeping,
and so softly you came knocking,
And so softly you came knocking,
knocking at my bedroom door,
That I could barely be certain I had heard you"
—at this point I threw the door wide open;—

Darkness there, and nothing more.

Deep into that darkness I gazed,
standing there for a long time wondering, fearing,
Questioning, imagining visions no human had
ever dared to envision before;
But the silence remained complete,
and the darkness offered no sign,
And the only word spoken
there was the whispered word, "Lenore!"
This I whispered, and an echo murmured
back the word, "Lenore!"

Merely this and nothing more.

Back into the room I turned,
my entire soul burning within me,
Soon I heard the tapping again,
this time somewhat louder than before.
"Surely," I said, "surely that is something
at my window lattice;
Let me see, then, what this is,
and explore this mystery—
Let my heart be quiet for a moment
and explore this mystery;—

"It's the wind and nothing more!"

I threw open the shutters,
and with much flapping and fluttering,
A majestic Raven from the sacred days of
long ago stepped inside.
He showed no respect whatsoever;
he didn't stop or pause for even a minute;
But, with the bearing of a lord or lady,
perched above my chamber door—
Perched on a bust of Pallas
just above my bedroom door—

Perched, and sat, and nothing more.

Then this black bird charmed my sorrowful thoughts
into smiling,
By the serious and solemn dignity
of the expression it displayed,
"Even though your head feathers are cut short
and shaved off,"
I said, "you are certainly no coward,
A terrifying, grim, and ancient raven
wandering from the nighttime shore,—
"Tell me what your noble name is on the Night's
Plutonian shore!"

"Nevermore," said the Raven.

I was amazed to hear
this awkward bird speak so clearly,
Though its answer carried little meaning
—little relevance it held;
For we cannot help but agree
that no living human being
Ever yet was blessed with seeing bird
above his chamber door—
Bird or beast perched on the carved bust
above his bedroom door,

With such name as "Nevermore."

But the Raven, sitting alone
on the calm bust, spoke only
That single word seemed to pour
out his entire soul.
Nothing more did he say
—not a feather did he move—
Until I barely whispered,
"Other friends have left before—"
"Tomorrow he will leave me,
just as my hopes have already disappeared."

Then the bird said, "Nevermore."

Shocked by the silence shattered by
such a perfectly timed response,
"Without a doubt," I said,
"what it speaks is all it knows and possesses,
Taken from some unfortunate owner
whom merciless Misfortune
Chased quickly and chased even faster
until all his songs carried the same message—
Until the funeral songs of his Hope
carried that sorrowful weight

Of 'Never—nevermore.'"

But the Raven still charmed
my sorrowful soul into smiling,
Immediately I rolled a cushioned chair
in front of the bird and the bust and the door;
Then, as I sank into the velvet,
I began connecting
Imagination upon imagination,
wondering what this foreboding bird
from ancient times—
What this dark, awkward, ghostly, thin and threatening
bird from long ago

Meant in croaking "Nevermore."

This I sat engaged in guessing,
but not expressing a single word
To the bird whose blazing eyes
now pierced straight into the depths of my heart;
This and more I pondered,
with my head comfortably resting back
On the cushion's velvet surface
that the lamplight gleamed upon,
But whose soft violet velvet lining
with the lamplight gleaming over

She will never press again!

Then, I thought, the air became thicker,
filled with fragrance from an invisible incense burner
Carried by angels whose footsteps
chimed softly on the cushioned floor.
"You miserable creature," I shouted,
"your God has given you—
through these angels he has sent you
Respite—
respite and nepenthe from thy memories of Lenore!
"Drink, oh drink this soothing potion,
and forget this lost Lenore!"

"Nevermore," said the Raven.

"Prophet!" I said, "creature of evil!
—prophet still, whether you are bird or devil!—
Whether you were sent by a tempter,
or whether a storm cast you here upon this shore,
Desolate yet completely fearless,
on this enchanted desert land—
On this home haunted by horror—
tell me the truth, I beg you—
"Is there—is there balm in Gilead?
—tell me—tell me, I beg you!"

"Nevermore," said the Raven.

"Prophet!" I said, "creature of evil
—prophet still, whether you're bird or devil!"
By the Heaven that arches above us
—by the God we both worship—
Tell this grief-stricken soul whether,
in the far-off paradise,
It will embrace a holy maiden whom the angels call
Lenore—
"Embrace a rare and radiant maiden
whom the angels call Lenore."

"Nevermore," said the Raven.

"Let that word be our sign of farewell,
bird or demon!" I screamed, jumping up—
"Get back into the storm
and the dark shores of the underworld!"
Leave no dark feather as a sign of the lie
your soul has told!
"Leave my loneliness unbroken!
—quit the bust above my door!"
"Take your beak from out my heart,
and take your form from off my door!"

"Nevermore," said the Raven.

And the Raven, never flitting,
still is sitting, still is sitting
On the pale marble bust of Pallas
positioned just above my bedroom door;
And his eyes appear to hold all the qualities
of a demon lost in dreams,
And the lamplight streaming over him
casts his shadow on the floor;
And my soul from out that shadow
that lies floating on the floor

Shall be lifted—nevermore!

Thank You For Reading

You've Just Read a Piece of the Greatest Library Ever Rebuilt

Thank you for reading.

This book is one of thousands we're restoring, reimagining, and translating as part of the **Modern Library of Alexandria** — a global movement to preserve and share humanity's most important ideas.

What was once lost to fire and time is now rising again — not just as memory, but as living, breathing knowledge, freely accessible to all.

What You Can Do Next:

- **Keep Reading.**

  Discover more legendary works — in beautiful print, audiobook, or digital form — at LibraryofAlexandria.com.

- **Build Your Own Library.**

  Every title is available as a paperback, hardcover, or collectible boxset — at true printing cost. Craft a personal library worthy of display.

- **Spread the Light.**

  Share this book. Tell others about the movement. Help us translate every timeless work into every language, so no reader is ever left behind.

By finishing this book, you've already taken part in something extraordinary.

Join us at LibraryofAlexandria.com

Together, we're rebuilding the greatest library the world has ever known.

With appreciation,

The Modern Library of Alexandria Team

Visit:
www.libraryofalexandria.com
Or scan the code below:

www.ingramcontent.com/pod-product-compliance
Lightning Source LLC
Chambersburg PA
CBHW010139030826
48979CB00023B/1032

* 9 7 8 1 8 0 6 6 8 0 7 3 3 *